Don't Worry Bear

Don't Worry Bear

by Greg Foley

VIKING

For friends who are there

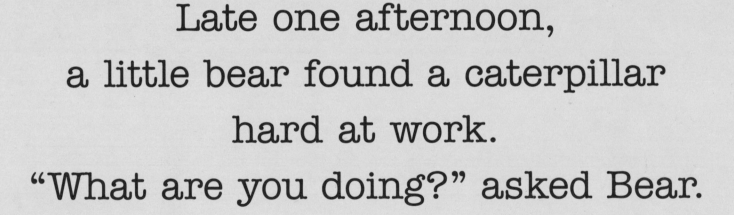

Late one afternoon,
a little bear found a caterpillar
hard at work.
"What are you doing?" asked Bear.

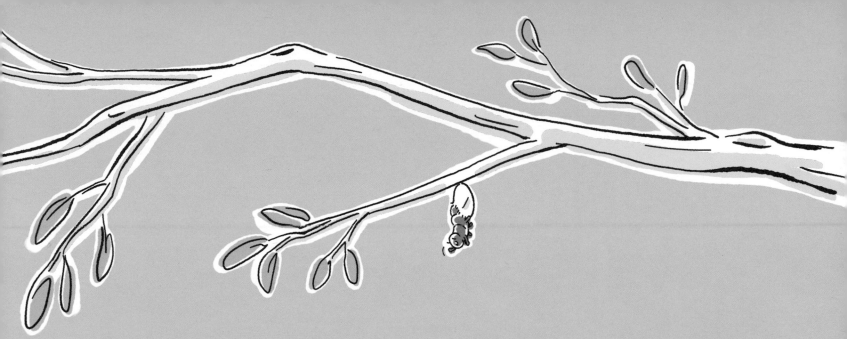

"I'm making a cocoon,"
said Caterpillar.
"I'll stay inside for a while.
But I promise you'll see me again."

That night, Bear got worried.
He came to check the cocoon.
Caterpillar said, "Don't worry, Bear.
I'm not afraid of the dark."

He came again on a windy day.
Caterpillar said, "Don't worry, Bear.
A little wind doesn't bother me."

He came when it rained.
Caterpillar said, "Don't worry, Bear.
I'm not getting wet."

He came when it got cold.
Caterpillar said, "Don't worry, Bear.
I'm very warm and cozy."

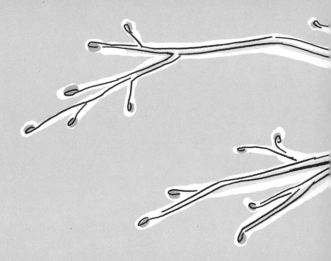

He brought Mouse to see the cocoon.
Mouse said, "Don't worry, Bear.
I think Caterpillar's sleeping."

The little bear stopped worrying
about Caterpillar.

Until...

Bear found the cocoon empty.
Then he started worrying
all over again.

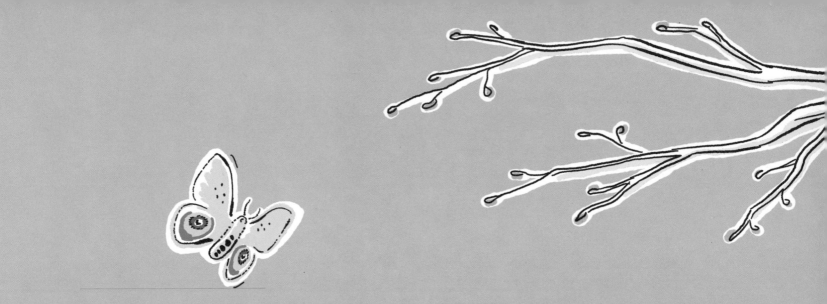

While Bear was worrying,
a beautiful silk moth fluttered by.
Bear said, "Caterpillar is gone.
I'm afraid I'll never see him again."

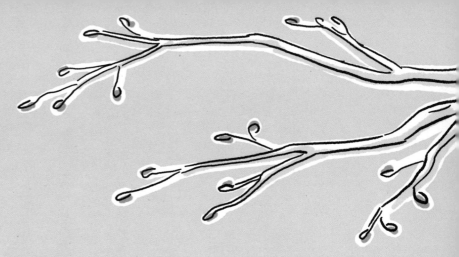

Then the silk moth landed
on Bear's paw.
"Don't worry, Bear," he said.

"I'm right here!"

VIKING
Published by Penguin Group
Penguin Young Readers Group, 345 Hudson Street, New York, New York 10014, U.S.A.
Penguin Group (Canada), 90 Eglinton Avenue East, Suite 700, Toronto, Ontario, Canada M4P 2Y3
(a division of Pearson Penguin Canada Inc.)

Penguin Books Ltd, Registered Offices: 80 Strand, London WC2R 0RL, England

First published in 2008 by Viking, a division of Penguin Young Readers Group

1 3 5 7 9 10 8 6 4 2

LIBRARY OF CONGRESS CATALOGING-IN-PUBLICATION DATA
Foley, Greg E.
Don't worry Bear / by Greg Foley.
p. cm.
Summary: A caterpillar reassures a worried bear that they will see each other again
when the caterpillar emerges from its cocoon.
ISBN 978-0-670-06245-4 (hardcover)
[1. Bears—Fiction. 2. Cocoons. 3. Caterpillars—Fiction. 4. Butterflies—Fiction.]
I. Title. II. Title: Do not worry Bear.
PZ7.F35Do 2008
[E]—dc22
2007024253

Manufactured in China
Set in American Typewriter Regular

This book was printed using chlorine-free Greenery FSC & Recycled Paper,
an environmentally friendly paper from Austria that contains 70% recycled materials
(66.5% post-consumer waste, 3.5% pre-consumer waste).
This paper is certified by the Forest Stewardship Council.